The Cat's Meow

BY GARY SOTO

Illustrated by Joe Cepeda

A
LITTLE APPLE
PAPERBACK

SCHOLASTIC INC.
New York Toronto London Auckland Sydney

For Pip,
who once said
"Mama."

ISBN 0-590-47002-7

Text copyright © 1987 by Gary Soto.
Illustrations copyright © 1995 by Scholastic Inc.
All rights reserved. Published by Scholastic Inc., by arrangement with
Strawberry Hill Press, Portland, Oregon.

24 23 22 21 20 19 18 17   2   7 8 9/0

Printed in the U.S.A   40

CHAPTER
1

One Saturday morning Pip, our cat, came inside the house, looked at her empty bowl, and said, "Quiero más,* Graciela." With her paw, she pushed the bowl across the kitchen floor.

I happened to be in the kitchen studying the school menu, which was stuck on the refrigerator door. I looked down at Pip, amazed.

* I want more.

"¿Qué?" I asked. "What did you say?"

Pip said, "Meow." She touched her bowl with a paw. "Meow, meow."

But I knew she had said something — and I knew it wasn't English because I'm Mexican and it sounded like Spanish. I got down on my knees, took her furry head in my hands, and pleaded for her to talk, to say "Hola,"* Adiós,"** "Vamos a comer"*** — anything! But Pip only pulled away from my grip and raced to the front door. I let her out and watched her cross the street.

I went back inside to study the menu to see which lunches to buy for the coming week. (My mom lets me buy lunches twice a week, and sometimes three if there's really something special.) I circled "tuna boats" and "frankfurter boats," which sounded good even though I'd never heard of them

* Hello
** Good-bye
*** Let's go eat.

3

before. Then I went to my bedroom to read and wait for my mom and dad, who had gone to the store. (Now that I am a third grader they sometimes let me stay by myself.) But I couldn't concentrate. I kept wondering if she had really talked, or if I was just making it all up.

I heard our car drive in. I jumped off the bed and ran to the door. Dad was standing by the trunk, with Mom piling bags in his arms. I went outside to help.

"Hi, Mom, may I be your helper?"

Mom, who is a little hard of hearing, turned to Dad and asked, "What helper? Did we hire a helper?"

Dad, who is even more hard of hearing, said, "Yes, once when I was a boy I helped an old lady across the street."

And both of them are a little strange. Maybe it's because they're parents.

While the two of them put away the groceries I sat at the kitchen table wondering how to explain to them that Pip had talked.

4

I thought and thought. I couldn't figure out how to tell them. I decided for the moment not to say anything.

Instead, I went outside. Pip was on the porch, curled up in a streak of sunlight. I jumped up and sat on the railing, and ran my hands through her fur. I tugged a few loose pieces and threw them into the air. The wind caught the fur and jerked them around, lifting them higher beyond my reach or the reach even of a grown-up.

"¡Ay Ay Ay!"* said Pip, raising her head.

I jumped off the rail. "You're doing it again."

Pip blinked her eyes, sniffed the air, and placed her head back down between her paws.

"Pip! What did you say?" I tapped her head lightly, and she raised her head and looked at me. She stood up, arched her back, and yawned wide enough to let me see the be-

* Oh!

ginning of her throat. She stretched and said, "Meow."

"Pip, quit fooling around." I was mad, then suddenly frightened, because I was sure I had heard her say something that was human. But who would ever believe me? I was only eight-and-a-half, and small for my age. People would just say, "Sure, kid," and roll their eyes toward the ceiling.

I picked up Pip and held her in my arms. "Come on, you're mi gatito.* What did you say?"

Pip jumped from my arms, and before I knew it she was leaping from the rail onto the lawn. By the time I had run down the steps, she was across the street.

She looked back at me. "Adíos," she said, and headed for some bushes and a neighbor's yard. I went back inside. My parents were on the couch reading the newspaper. I climbed onto the couch and sat between

* my kitty

them. Not knowing how to start, I played with my fingers. I was bursting to tell them that Pip had said "Adios," but they didn't want me to bother them while they were reading.

Then suddenly, out of the blue, Mom started talking about when she was a little girl and used to go swimming at The Plunge. Dad shook his head and told me when he was a little girl he had a pool in his backyard.

"A little girl?" I asked.

"No, I'm Dad, and this is Mom," Dad said.

Crazy parents, I thought. I got up and went outside to see if Pip was around.

I couldn't find Pip but I did run into a friend skating by. It was Juanita, a fourth grader from school. I decided to tell her about Pip.

"Hey, Juanita," I shouted. "Guess what!"

She twirled around on her skates and stopped. "What?"

"Do you know any cats that can talk?" I

asked. Immediately I felt stupid. Of course she didn't. I mean I had never heard of such a thing, so why should she?

"Cats . . . talking? What are you . . . loca*?" she asked, squinching up her face.

"No. Pip can really talk."

"Have your head checked," she said, twirled on her skates, and started off. She didn't look back even when I shouted that, really, I had heard a cat talk, honest, I'll show you.

I spent the rest of the morning looking for Pip, only to return home, depressed that she was nowhere to be found. Or so I thought. When I went inside, I found her on my bed. I should have guessed. She likes my bed, and my parents' bed — or any bed, I guess. I approached her slowly, thinking that she might run away. But she only yawned when I stroked her back. She's soft,

* crazy

8

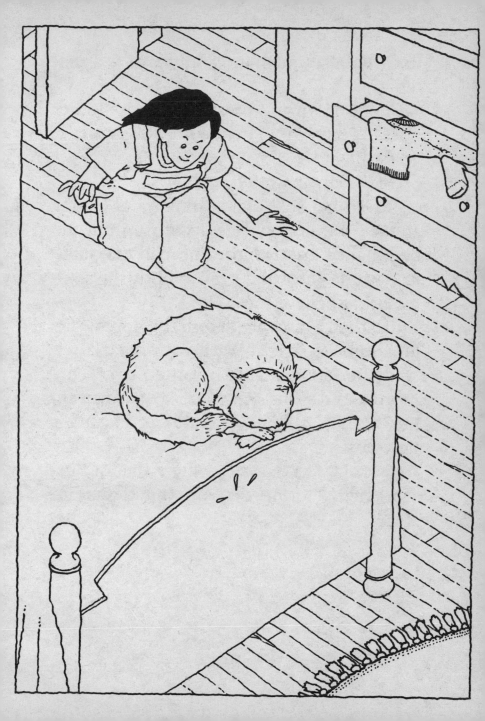

thick with so much fur, and warm as a mitten.

I bent down and pressed my nose to her nose. "Pretty Pip," I cooed. "You can talk, verdad*?"

"Sí,"** Pip answered.

"I told her so," I said, thinking of Juanita and her big smirky face. I got up from the bed, hands on my hips, and mad that Juanita — and probably everybody else — wouldn't believe me.

Just then Mom called from the porch, "It's lunchtime, Graciela. Wash your hands."

At the kitchen table I wanted to tell my mom and dad that Pip could speak Spanish, but both of them were still reading their newspapers.

"Mom," I said, swallowing a bite of tuna sandwich, "Mom, do you think cats are smart?"

* Isn't that true?
** Yes

"Ummmumm," she said without looking up from her newspaper.

"Do you think they can be trained?"

"Ummumm."

"Do you know that Pip can talk Spanish?"

"Ummumm." She turned the page. She looked up and pointed to my milk. "If you want to grow, you're going to have to drink your milk."

I was mad at my mom. She hadn't heard one word I had said. "Well, how much will I grow if I drink the whole carton?"

Mom thought a moment. "That's really a good question. You have such a curious mind."

I drank my milk, ate my sandwich, and licked the flakes of potato chips that had stuck to my fingers. That was the best part of lunch. I returned to my room and closed my door. Pip was still on my bed.

"Pip, my parents never listen."

Pip opened her sleeping eyes and said, "Qué lástima," and closed them very slowly.

"You can say that again," I answered back, and she did — and more. "Qué lástima. Tus papás actúan raro cuando leen el periódico."*

Yeah. Mom and Dad are weird.

* What a shame. Your parents get weird when they read the newspaper.

CHAPTER
2

After lunch I went over to Juanita's house, and called, "Juanita! Juanita! It's me!"

She came outside and stood on the porch. She shaded her brow and, after a long time, said, "Oh, hi, Graciela." She walked down the porch steps. "What's your cat up to? Is she in college yet?"

"No, but she's in this bag. Do you want to see her?"

"Yeah, why not." Juanita walked over

slowly, even though I knew she was anxious for a look.

I opened the paper shopping bag. Pip blinked at Juanita. Juanita made a face at Pip. "Okay, cat, what's up?"

"Meow," Pip said.

"Let's get those lips going," Juanita shot back.

"Meow," Pip repeated. "Meow, meow." She leaped gingerly out of the bag, stretched so that her fur stood up, and rubbed her head against my leg.

"Come on, Pip," I begged. "Por favor,* say something — anything!"

"Meow."

"I'll give you a can of tuna."

"Meow."

"Oh, Pip, quit fooling around."

"Meow, meow-meow," she said, and dashed away without even looking back.

Juanita shook her head. "Graciela, you're as crazy as your mom and dad."

* Please

"Really, she says lots of things."

Juanita turned away and walked up the porch. She stopped at the top step and turned around. "Graciela, you're double crazy."

That night for dinner we had huachinango,* a Veracruz seafood dish. My parents had put away their newspaper and magazines and were talking to me. It was strange being talked to.

"What would you like for your birthday, cupcakes or a cake?" my mom asked.

My birthday was a month away, and I was going to be nine, which meant of course that I could have nine friends over, no fewer and no more.

"Cupcakes," I said. "And I want them different colors, like red and blue and like that."

"When I was a girl, I liked cake better," Mom said.

* red snapper (a fish)

"Me, too," Dad said. "When I was a girl my mom made me a white cake with three layers."

"When you were a girl?" I asked, screwing up my face.

"No, I'm Dad," said Dad. He bit into his fish and chewed loudly.

This was our dinner conversation.

After dinner I found Pip on the back steps. She was sitting facing away from me, and when she heard me, she looked over her shoulder and said, "Tengo hambre."*

"Yeah, I thought you would be hungry. I brought you this." I held out a strip of fish skin. She sniffed it, poked her nose at it, and then delicately pulled it from my out-stretched palm. As she ate, I raked my hand through her fur, which was dusty and warm.

When she finished, she said, "Este pescado está muy sabroso."**

"Pip," I asked, "how did you learn how

* I'm hungry.
** This fish is very tasty.

17

to talk? Come on, be a friend and tell me."
I thought a moment, then added, "I'll get
you a can of tuna."

Pip looked skyward, thinking whether she
should. Then, licking her mouth, she nodded her head yes.

I scrambled to my feet and went inside.
Mom and Dad were on the couch staring at
the fireplace (which was not lit). Boy, I
thought, they're so strange. At least they
could watch TV like other parents.

I quietly took the can opener from the
drawer and a can of tuna from the pantry,
and hurried outside. "Muy bien,"* Pip said,
and followed me in a happy cat-prance, her
eyes on the tuna can, as we went to hide
under the apple tree.

As I struggled to open the tuna (I have no
muscles whatsoever and until then had
never used a can opener), Pip began to tell
me her story.

* Very well.

18

First she told me that she also belonged to someone else. This sort of shocked me. I mean, I thought she was my cat. Her other owner lived around the corner in a house that was painted half yellow and half blue.

"Mi otro amo es el señor Medina."*

"Oh, I know him," I said. "He's sort of . . . different?"

"No, el señor es una persona inteligente." Pip gave me a stern look, a look so stern I had to look away. "Silencio, por favor."**

I let Pip continue telling her story. She said that she started going over to Sr.*** Medina's when we — Dad, Mom, and I — went on a vacation for two weeks. We had arranged for a student (my dad's a teacher at the high school) to take care of Pip, but the student hardly ever showed up. When he did, he only sat around the house with the stereo turned up loud as he watered the plants. But

* My other master is Mr. Medina.
** No, he's an intelligent person. Silence, please.
*** Mr.

he never fed Pip. Pip would meow, scream, roll onto her back, scratch the furniture, but for some reason he never bothered to feed her. And Pip figured out why. He didn't know that the box of cat food was inside the dryer. (We keep her food there because Pip will eat until she is as fat as a pig if we don't stop her.)

On the fourth day Pip didn't bother to come back home. She decided to run away because she was mad at us for leaving her with such an idiot. She crossed the street and cut through a yard to Sr. Medina's back porch, where she meowed long and hard until he came out.

"¿Qué tal, gatito blanco?"* Sr. Medina asked in a friendly voice.

Pip described how he picked her up, patted her head, and took her inside, where there were books everywhere: on the stove, on the windowsills, piled in front of the window, tottering in crooked walls.

* What's up, little white kitty?

Sr. Medina was a smart man who was trying to get smarter by reading 10,000 books. When Pip came by that day, he was on book 8,329, so he was pretty smart. He spoke seven languages, one for each day of the week. That day, a Tuesday, was his Spanish day. Wednesday was Italian day, Thursday was German, and so on.

Pip was about to tell me how she learned Spanish when we heard the porch door slam and Mom call, "Graciela, get your coat. We're going somewhere."

Pip had to stop telling me (just at the good part!) how at night Sr. Medina would put earphones on her, so that she could listen to a Spanish station until morning. Pip said the words just sank into her brain.

Even though I wanted to stay, I went with Mom and Dad, who, to my dissatisfaction, decided to walk to the ice cream shop instead of drive. I pretended to limp, so that Dad would go get the car, but neither of my parents even noticed. At the shop my mouth began to water. I love ice cream, and my favorite is bubble-gum ice cream.

As we sat on the bench outside the store, I noticed that my parents were holding hands. How cute, I thought. They're so old and they still like that kind of stuff.

But when I looked closer, I noticed that their hands were dripping with ice cream. A big puddle began to spread on the ground. I looked up. Their faces were smeared with ice cream, and Mom even had some on her eyelashes!

On the way back home (they were still holding hands and the ice cream was now smeared along their throats), I decided to ask if they had ever heard of a talking cat.

"Sure, I like cats," my mom said.

"Me, too, mi'ja,"* Dad chimed in.

I shook my head and shrugged my shoulders. They were not listening. I tried again.

* my daughter

"Do you know if scientists can teach animals to talk?"

"Yes, it would be great, Graciela, if you became a scientist."

"Yes, you could help the world."

Chihuahua, I thought, they're beyond help. I rolled my eyes skyward and shook my head.

CHAPTER
3

Once we were on our block, I raced home, leaving my parents behind. I went to the backyard, where I found Pip drinking water from our pond.

Both of us settled again in our hideout under the apple tree, and Pip began where she left off.

Night after night Sr. Medina put earphones on her head to listen to the Spanish station. Within a month she knew a lot of Spanish. But at first she had trouble talking

because her tongue was not used to forming words. Sr. Medina helped by carefully pulling on her tongue and stretching her mouth so that the words could come out freely. This was the trick he used on himself when he learned Russian.

Mom called me to come in. I got up, hooked the can opener on my belt, pulled out my shirt so that she wouldn't see it, and went inside with Pip following me. And just as I got into the kitchen, the can opener fell out.

Mom picked up the can opener and exclaimed, "Oh, good, we can have dessert now."

"No, we already *had* dessert," I said.

"Well, we'll have some more."

So I ate a bowl of fruit cocktail, took a bath, and, when my parents were not looking, sneaked Pip into my bed.

When Mom came to give me a good-night kiss, Pip became absolutely still. Mom kissed both sides of my face and my forehead three times. And just as Mom was leaving, Pip said, "Buenas noches."*

Mom turned around. "Did you say something?"

"No."

She shrugged her shoulders and left. Pip came out from under the covers and started walking on my chest. I giggled, then laughed out loud.

* Good night.

28

Mom warned me from the living room, "You better go to sleep. Sleep makes the brain grow."

But I couldn't stop laughing. Pip was now pawing my stuffed animals, jumping up and down on them.

"¡Fíjate!* I'm telling you, you better be quiet," Mom said, her tone now more serious.

"Yes, it's better to be quiet when you sleep," said You-Know-Who.

I woke with Pip sniffing my ear and poking around my neck. I giggled and squirmed.

"It's tickling!" I pushed her away, slipped into my slippers, and took a peek into my parents' bedroom. Dad was sleeping with the covers around his feet; Mom was snoring like a saw. Great, I said to myself. I closed the door and went to the kitchen. When I opened the refrigerator, Pip jumped off my bed and hurried over to take a look. She pointed to a hamburger patty.

* Pay attention!

"Yeah, that sounds good." I took it out and placed it in the microwave oven.

"Es para mí, ¿verdad?"*

I looked down at Pip. She rolled onto her back and patted her stomach. I was really planning to eat it (I love hamburgers, especially in the morning), but I decided on a trade.

"Okay, I'll let you have it, but only if you tell me even more about how you learned to talk."

Pip rolled off her back in a flash.

While we ate (I had cereal), Pip told me how she and Sr. Medina played tricks on the mailman and door-to-door salesmen and anyone who came to his house. He would stand on the porch with Pip at his feet, saying things like "Hi! How you doin'?" "Boy, it's a beautiful day." "Oh, good, the book has finally arrived." While he made small talk, Pip mimicked him, saying things like, "¡Hola señor cartero!" "¿Cómo está?" "Qué bonito

* It's for me, right?

31

está el día, no le parece?" "¡Al fin llegó mi libro!"* It amazed those people who came over. They didn't know where that other voice had come from as they looked around, puzzled.

I stopped Pip. "Pip, I want to meet Sr. Medina."

Pip thought for a long time. "Es posible, pero quiero otra lata de atún."**

"¡Orale!"*** We shook hands, I mean paws, or whatever. I opened another can of tuna, and was setting it down for her to eat when I heard Mom and Dad stir in bed.

Pip and I scooted out of the house with the can of tuna as quickly as we could.

"Graciela," I heard my mom say. I went back inside.

"Graciela," I heard my dad say, rubbing his sleepy eyes.

"Did you have breakfast yet?" Mom asked

* Hello, Mr. Mailman. How are you? It's a beautiful day, don't you think? At last you brought my book!
** It's possible, but I want another can of tuna.
*** All right!

as she set the kettle on the stove for coffee.

"Yeah, Pip and I . . ." I started. "I mean, yeah, I ate the leftover hamburger in the fridge."

"The hamburger?" Mom asked, her face screwed up.

"The hamburger?" Dad echoed as he pulled the sports section from the morning paper and staggered sleepily to the kitchen table.

While Mom started frying chorizo,* I stuck my head out of the back door. "See you in a little while. I have to eat breakfast with them." Pip looked up from her licked-clean tuna can. "And you better hide that can," I warned her. Pip poked it with her nose and rolled it toward the apple tree.

While we had breakfast I tried to make conversation, but my parents were already lost to the newspaper.

"Dad, Pip can talk."

"That's wonderful that you like to read."

* Mexican sausage

33

"Mom, Sr. Medina taught Pip Spanish."

"Great, I'll call Eva's mother about going swimming."

"Mom and Dad, you're both crazy."

"Your papi and me are happy you made your bed."

When I finished breakfast, I started to hurry outside but was told to come back in to clear the table. It's strange. My parents never seem to listen to me, but they know when I'm going to have fun and always spoil it by making me do chores.

CHAPTER
4

When the table was cleared, I ran outside without even saying good-bye, and without missing a beat Pip wheeled onto her hind legs and chased me to Sr. Medina's house. He was in the front yard, watering his flowers.

"¿Cómo está usted?"* I said, greeting him with a smile.

* How are you?

"¿Cómo te va, niña?"* he answered back. He seemed a little puzzled. He looked at Pip, then me. "¿Cómo te llamas?"**

"Graciela," I said. "I live on the next block." I pointed in the direction of my house. "Can you see where that tall tree is? Well, I don't live *there* but just next door."

Pip leaped onto his white picket fence.

"Sr. Medina," I said, "Pip told me the whole thing. I mean, she told me you taught her how to talk." I turned to Pip. "Huh, Pip?"

Pip meowed and rubbed her shoulder against a picket.

"Isn't that right?" I asked again.

Pip meowed twice.

"Come on, tell Sr. Medina the truth!"

Pip meowed three times.

What was going on? I wondered. "Come on, Pip, don't play games. Say something!"

Just then Juanita came skating by. I dreaded this. I knew she was going to act

* How are you doing, little girl?
** What's your name?

37

smart. She barked at Pip and yelled, "Is your cat talking French now?" She made an ugly face by pushing her tongue into the space between her teeth. She laughed and skated away.

I couldn't believe it. Pip wouldn't talk and Sr. Medina pretended not to even know Pip.

"That's a pretty cat you have," he finally said. "What's his name?"

"HER," I almost shouted. "You know very well who she is! You taught her how to talk!"

"I did, did I?" He widened his eyes in surprise and laughed. "Whatever you say is okay with me." As he walked away he chuckled, "A talking cat!"

I watched Pip trot away gingerly on the fence, with what looked like a big smile on her face. "Pip, I'm mad at you." Then I told her in Spanish, "Pip, estoy furiosa contigo."*

Pip jumped off the fence and ran across the street. I ran home and cried in my room. I felt like a big fool.

* Pip, I'm furious with you.

Since it was Sunday, Mom and Dad decided to take a drive to Big Rock, which, if you want to know the truth, is only a small rock. I can climb it easily; Dad can climb it, too, but usually he rips his pants or scrapes his hands or slides back down, screaming for help. Sometimes little kids have to pick him up.

The Sunday drive made me feel better. It took my mind off Pip and her Big Fat Lie. But back at home I began to think and think and think about Pip. No one else seemed to hear Pip talk. Maybe I was going crazy. But all I had to do was sit down with my parents for dinner to decide who was crazy.

"Pip can be our guide if we go to Spain," I said, while tearing into my enchilada.

"That's good, now all you have to do is pick up your clothes after dinner," Mom said.

"Pip's going to teach us Spanish guitar," I said to Dad, who had a bandage on his head from a fall he took at Big Rock.

"Great! Maybe one of your friends would like to go hiking with us next week."

"You're both crazy," I said, rolling my eyes to the ceiling.

"Yeah, let's go out for ice cream tonight," Mom said.

"Yeah, ice cream," Dad said with his mouth full.

What can you do with parents like this?

The next day, Monday, I slinked to school hoping that Juanita hadn't said anything to anyone. But she had. There were some snickering kids by the monkey bars going, "Meow, meow, meow."

Feeling embarrassed, I hurried to my classroom and for the whole day kept hearing inside my head, "Meow, meow, meow." Then, toward the end of the schoolday, a boulder of anger began to roll inside of me. I began to think that Pip wasn't my friend. Why would she trick me like that? Sr. Medina hadn't taught her how to speak Spanish. She was a big liar.

*   *   *

After school I stomped home, put on my play clothes, and went outside to search for Pip. She hadn't returned home the previous night. Lucky for her. I probably would have strangled her. Well, maybe not. That would have just made me feel even worse.

I went out to the porch. "Pip," I called.

I looked in the backyard, in the apple tree, and even under the house. I came out dusty and sneezing. Mom was in the backyard beating the laundry on the line. She thinks it makes the clothes dry faster.

"Mom, have you seen Pip?" I asked.

"Yes, it's lovely weather," she answered.

"No, Mom, HAVE YOU SEEN PIP?"

"We're having pork chops tonight."

Boy, I thought, what a mom. I left yelling, "Pip, ¿dónde estás?"*

I went to the front yard and searched the bushes. I only saw snails looking at me, and spotted a ball I had lost last winter.

"Pip," I yelled. "Pip, can you hear me?"

* Pip, where are you?

41

"Hola, mi amiga,"* a voice said.

I squinted my eyes at the camellia bush. "Pip, come out!"

She was sitting on a high branch, her paws pressed together, and smiling.

I climbed the camellia and tapped her on the head meanly. "Why did you fool me like that?"

Pip explained that it was my fault. Sr. Medina would have told me that he had taught Pip how to talk, would have told me everything, except that I had blabbed my big mouth in public. Someone could have heard me, and ruined everything for Sr. Medina.

Oh, I said to myself. I felt stupid. A talking cat is something very rare. I mean, you just can't go blabbing that your pet can speak.

"I'm sorry, Pip," I said, petting her. "I should have guessed."

"Está bien, amiguita."** Pip rubbed against my shoulder and purred.

* Hi, my friend.
** It's all right, little friend.

42

Pip jumped down and trotted in the direction of Sr. Medina's. I followed her, excited at the possibility of seeing him. He was on the front porch, an empty glass of lemonade at his feet. He rose and greeted me.

"Ven acá, muchacha."* He beckoned me. "Your name's Graciela, que no?"** He hesitated a moment, then said, "Pip has told me about you. ¿Verdad, Pip?"***

"Sí. Esta niñita es mi amiga y yo la quiero mucho."****

I couldn't believe it. They were talking. I felt strange, like the first time I rode a Ferris wheel. Everything seemed to turn this way and that way.

"Come up on the porch. I don't want anyone to see us."

I looked over my shoulder. There was a

* Come here, little girl.
** right?
*** Right, Pip?
**** Yes. This little girl is my friend and I love her a lot.

neighbor watering the strip of lawn along the curb. Was she watching us? Her head, shaded by a goofy straw hat, was certainly turned our way. As I hurried up the steps, I realized that I had seen that woman before — right in my backyard! She's the neighborhood snoop who spreads lies and gossip — chisme.* Once she even had the nerve to peek over our fence when we were having a fiesta.**

Sr. Medina didn't have to be warned about this snoop. She had been watching his house for over a year.

After a while, we got up and went inside the house.

Pip was right. There were books everywhere, stacked in corners and tottering in high and short piles right in the middle of the living room. Dust lay like a shadow over everything, and a huge, black, creepy spider

* gossip
** party, celebration

44

sat curiously on one of those school globes. When it moved, I stepped back, scared.

"How do you like it?" Sr. Medina asked. He chuckled to himself. "That's Pete, a desert tarantula. I guess you can say he's my pet."

"Can he talk, too?"

"Oh, no," Sr. Medina said. "His brain is not developed the way yours and mine are — or Pip's. But he can do other things we can't do. Like live without water for ninety days, and poison a mouse and eat it. I can't do that, can you?"

"No, and I'm glad. I would never eat a mouse."

Sr. Medina chuckled. "You might . . . if you were hungry enough." He pointed to a chair. "Siéntate."*

I sat down in an overstuffed chair, but stood up quickly because I realized I had sat on Pip, who was curled there.

"Perdón,** Pip, I didn't see you."

* Sit down.
** I'm sorry.

"No importa,"* she said, raising her head. She winked at Sr. Medina and placed her head back down, and started to purr loudly on her journey to dreamland.

"Why do you read so much?" I asked, touching a dusty book.

"I want to know everything there is to know," he said. "If I live to be a hundred, I just might make it." He pointed to a book on the table. "I'm reading about Aztec astronomy — ¡fantástico!"**

I walked over to the table and was going to sit in one of the chairs when Sr. Medina said, "Oh, no, not that one."

"Why?" I asked. Then I looked down. My hair, which is long and nearly to the middle of my back, almost stood up when I saw a snake raise its diamond-shaped head. It looked at me with green eyes and pushed out a wiggly red tongue. I screamed and ran over to hug Pip.

* It doesn't matter.
** Fantastic!

Sr. Medina had picked up the snake. "He's a harmless fellow. I got him on a boat trip."

I shook my head and said, "No me gustan serpientes."* I didn't like that snake, or the tarantula. I didn't even care for the mice that lived in Mice City, which were rows and rows of matchbox houses. Some milk cartons were the skyscrapers where the mice worked. Sr. Medina was certainly an interesting man.

I left in a hurry, without Pip, who promised to return before nightfall.

The woman watering her lawn began to cackle; she took off her hat and wiped her brow. She was like a witch, with lots of moles on her chin and a big hangy nose and everything. Oh no, I thought to myself. She's going to blab around the neighborhood that she had seen me run from Sr. Medina's house. Maybe she knows that Pip can talk!

* I don't like snakes.

48

CHAPTER
5

I was too scared to think of the consequences. I ran with all my might and was so glad to see my house, and Mom in the front yard watering some dead flowers from last year.

"Hi," I said, out of breath. I thought a moment. Mom should know about Sr. Medina. That witch will probably come over and spread a bunch of lies about him. "You'll never believe who I met today, Mom."

"Yes, it's just lovely for April," she said.

"Míra,* look at those clouds, don't they remind you of something?" She pointed to a regular round, puffy cloud.

I studied the cloud, which was moving very slowly or perhaps not at all.

"It just looks like a cloud to me," I finally said.

"Oh, use your imagination, Graciela."

I looked at the cloud again. I couldn't guess what it looked like, but to humor my mom I took a wild guess and said, "An old broken-down truck?"

"Oh, you're absolutely right," Mom cried. "I tell you, our family is smart."

She laughed and sprayed the water skyward to make a rainbow and to get herself all wet.

"Mail for you," Mom sang out in the kitchen. I raced from my room to the kitchen, where on the table lay a package wrapped in brown

* Look

50

paper. I was surprised by this piece of mail. I almost never get any, except birthday cards from my grandparents and my aunts and uncles. I tore into the package and, to my shock, discovered a book: *Spanish Made Simple*.

"Look, Mom, it's a Spanish book."

"Terrific!" Mom said. "That's great!"

She came over and took a look. "It's lovely. Who gave it to you — tu abuelo*?"

There was no return address or stamps in the corner. This seemed unusual. The more I stared at the book (it was all dusty), the more I thought that it was from Sr. Medina. He must have dropped it in our mailbox the night before.

"No, it's from Sr. Medina," I said. I saw it was an opportunity to tell Mom about him. "I met him when Pip took me over to his house. Pip can speak Spanish, Mom."

"Yeah, Pip is a good cat."

* your grandfather

51

"Mom, you're not listening."

"What is it, honey?" she said, touching my shoulder.

"I said, Pip can talk, and talk in Spanish."

Mom looked at me for a long time right in the eyes, and then punched me softly on the arm. "You're just like your dad. What a beautiful imagination."

I rolled my eyes toward the ceiling. "Boy, I wish I had a brother," I muttered. "Then I know I could talk to someone in the family who made sense."

In my bedroom I thought and thought and thought about Sr. Medina, and realized that he was a nice man, a little strange, yes, but nice. So what if he has strange pets? One of my best friends has a pet snake, so what's wrong with an adult owning a snake?

"But why is he so different?" I said to my favorite stuffed animal, Dolphy (he's a dolphin).

Dolphy looked at me and said (I have to speak for him), "You're just a scaredy-cat."

"No I'm not!"

Dolphy shook his head at me and scolded. "Yes you are!"

He was right. I had to go back to Sr. Medina's. I had to find out more about him. He seemed nice, didn't he?

"Okay," I said. "I'll go but you're coming with me."

"No, I don't want to go," pleaded Dolphy. "I'm scared, too."

With Dolphy I hurried from my bedroom to the living room and was almost out the front door when Mom called me back.

"If you're going out to play, you better not go far." She was peeling a potato at the kitchen sink. "We're going to eat dinner early tonight."

I thought for a moment, finger on my chin. "Okay, I'll just be on the front lawn."

On the lawn I took off my sweater and hung it on a bush. "Mom will think this is me. She never notices me anyhow."

I raced to Sr. Medina's and found him in the driveway. He was fixing his car.

"Hi," I said shyly.

"Hola, Graciela," he said, wiping his hands on a rag. "I'm glad you came back. Come on inside for a bit."

"I'm sorry for running away, but I'm scared of snakes. And scared of a lot of things."

I jumped when I felt something rubbing against my leg. I looked down and discovered Pip. I got to my knees and petted her.

"¿Cómo estás?" she asked. "¿Cómo te ha ido?"*

Pip purred and ran a rough tongue across my wrist.

The three of us climbed the porch steps, Pip prancing ahead, and went into the living room. It was dark. The curtains were closed, with only a sliver of dusty light coming through. I examined a glass case filled with bugs and let the snake curl around my neck. "You sure have some strange things," I said when I spotted a boar's head on the wall.

* How are you? How have you been?

Sr. Medina laughed and started to dust his tarantula, Pete, who lifted a leg for the feather duster to pass under.

Then I remembered the book at home. "You sent me that Spanish book, didn't you?"

"Es un regalo,"* he said. "It might help when you converse with Pip."

"Claro que sí," Pip said. "En un mes vas a hablar como un profesor."**

"Maybe," I said, "but I already know a lot of Spanish."

"Qué bueno,"*** Sr. Medina said, shifting a pile of books from one place to another. "I've got to start cooking dinner."

"Wait a minute!" I said. I looked around to be sure that no one else was listening. "How did you *really* teach Pip how to talk? I want to know."

* It's a gift.
** Of course. In a month you're going to speak like a professor.
*** That's good.

He winked at me, and double winked at Pip, as he lugged his toolbox onto the porch. "It's something you have to figure out on your own."

"Well, Pip said that you put earphones on her and made her listen to the Spanish station."

"If Pip said that, then it must be true." He winked at Pip and Pip winked back.

I turned to Pip angrily. "And what else did he do?"

"No te puedo decir,"* Pip said.

"¿Por qué no?" I asked. "Díme, por favor."**

Pip ran toward the fence, climbed up, and, looking back, said, "Adiós, amigos. Ya me voy a mi otra casa."***

"Pip!" I screamed.

But she was gone. I turned back to Sr.

* I can't tell you.
** Why not? Tell me, please.
*** 'Bye, friends. I'm going to my other house now.

Medina. He was on the porch steps, unlacing his boots.

"Graciela, Pip and I have a secret. It's between her and me, and I'm sorry, it doesn't include you. It has to be that way."

He stood up with a tired grunt. "And now I want you to keep a secret for me. You can't say a word to your folks, or your friends at school, or anyone. This is our secret."

I looked down at the ground. I thought I should be hurt for being excluded, but strangely I wasn't. He was right. Why should Pip break a secret?

"Okay," I said.

"That's good," he said. "Buenas noches,* Graciela."

"But Sr. Medina," I begged, "could you tell me why you read so much?"

He turned around and gave me a warm look. "No more questions, Graciela. Adiós, niña."**

* Good night
** Good-bye, child.

CHAPTER
6

As I expected, Mom hadn't missed me. I took my sweater from the bush, went inside, and found Mom in the kitchen still peeling potatoes. There was a tall mound of them.

"What's for dinner?" I asked.

"You'll see," she answered.

That night we had potato pie, baked potatoes, potato salad, french fries, a green salad, and milk for me and a glass of wine for my parents.

"This is delicious," Dad exclaimed. "What is it?"

Mom blushed. "I can't let out a family secret."

At this, I thought it might be appropriate to ask a question.

"Mom, do you think that a secret is a secret?" I asked with a serious face. I was thinking of Sr. Medina.

"So you like this dinner, too," Mom said, waving her fork at me. Then she turned to Dad. "And, Dear! Graciela got a book from Grandpa today. It's a German lesson book."

"No, Mom," I argued. "It wasn't from Grandpa but from Sr. Medina on the next street. And it's Spanish!"

"Yes, from Grandpa Medina," Mom said.

Dad, who was peeling off the skin of a potato, asked, "Who is Grandpa Medina?"

"He's your father, you big silly head." Mom laughed and slapped her knees.

Dad chuckled into his napkin.

* * *

That night I waited for Pip, but she didn't return home. The next day at first recess I had to suffer teasing from Juanita and her gang, but toward the end of the day they left me alone.

When I got home I found Mom in the kitchen slicing tomatoes. Oh boy, I thought, what could she possibly be making?

"Hi, Mom," I greeted her. "Have you seen Pip?"

"Pip?" Her face darkened with lines as she thought. "No, I haven't seen her."

I couldn't believe it. For the first time in a long time I got a straight answer from her.

I changed into my play clothes, threw my sweater on the bush outside, and ran over to Sr. Medina's house. I couldn't believe my eyes. There were television crews swarming like ants over one another, cables running every which way, and reporters shooting pictures. One reporter had climbed the telephone pole for a better view. His hat fell off his head and fluttered in the air.

A burly policeman guarded Sr. Medina's gate.

I ran up to him. "Hey, what's going on?"

He looked down at me. His face was red and sweaty. "It sounds crazy to me, but they say that this guy — what's his name, Medina? — has taught a cat how to talk. It sounds darn crazy."

"Did you say *talk?*"

"Yeah, talk."

"Do you mean talk, TALK?"

"Yes, TALK TALK!"

The policeman turned and yelled at a reporter who was standing on the fence pointing his camera at the house.

The reporter lost his balance and fell into a bush. He needed help getting out.

"Geemenese!" the policeman yelled. While he went over to help, I sneaked through the side hedge and raced to the back porch. I knocked and whispered, "Sr. Medina, it's me, Graciela."

I knocked and whispered, knocked and

whispered. Finally Sr. Medina unlatched the screen door to let me in.

"Hola, little one," he said in a low, sorrowful voice, and turned away to walk back into the kitchen.

What was wrong? Wasn't he glad to see me? He looked sad. Then it hit me, like one of Sr. Medina's big books fallen off the shelf. Maybe he thought I was the one who had broken the secret and told everyone that Pip could talk.

I followed him to the living room, where we sat in silence.

Feeling bad, I decided to ask Sr. Medina. "Do you think I told them?" I pointed to the crowd outside, which had grown larger and noisier and more eager to race onto the porch, bang on the door, and demand answers about the talking cat.

"I know it wasn't you," he said. He ran his hands through his hair and looked in the direction of the crowd. "It was la viega*

* the old lady

64

across the street. Remember the one who was watering her lawn?"

I nodded. I knew she was the one who had blabbed.

"She called the newspapers about Pip," he said. He thought a moment, then added, "Why can't people let other people be?"

Sr. Medina sat wearily in his chair. Wanting to prove I was tough, I sat down in the same chair where the snake had been. I held my breath, hoping that it wasn't there. And thank God it wasn't.

"Yes," Sr. Medina said, "she's been watching me for months." He turned his face to mine. "You know, Graciela, I have traveled all over the world, and wherever I've gone, it's been the same story. People just like to talk even when they don't have a darn thing to say."

I gazed down at the floor and played with my fingers. I raised my head and asked, "What are you going to do?"

"No sé,"* he said. (Now that I look back,

* I don't know.

I know Sr. Medina knew what he was going to do but didn't want to tell me.)

Pip walked into the living room. She seemed sad.

"¿Estás triste?"* I asked as she jumped into my lap and nuzzled her head under my chin.

"Sí,"** she said.

I hugged Pip and whispered, "Poor Sr. Medina. Poor all of us."

Sr. Medina rose with a sigh and said that I should leave. "I have to deal with these people. They're in love with gossip, the whole world is in love with chisme."

"Oh, I feel bad," I said. "They've ruined everything."

"No te preocupes,*** Graciela, it'll turn out just fine. You'll see."

I got up slowly, shook hands with Sr.

* Are you sad?
** Yes.
*** Don't worry

66

Medina, and left by climbing the back fence. Pip followed me for a while, but then disappeared.

"Pip," I called. "Come back, por favor."

I called and called until it was almost dark.

That night we had tomato cakes, stewed tomatoes, a green salad that was mostly tomatoes, and (I couldn't drink mine) tomato juice.

"Dear, you're so magical," Dad said with red stains around his mouth. "How do you do it?"

"It's an old family secret," Mom said, blushing. She waved her fork, which was stuck with a tomato. Picking up his cue, Dad waved his fork at her as he pretended he was a conductor of a symphony.

I felt sad. I played with my dinner but couldn't eat. Sr. Medina believed me, didn't he?

That night I watched the news on television, and sure enough, there was a segment on Sr. Medina. There was a crowd in front of his house, people standing on the fence and yelling for him to show them the talking cat. A reporter on the scene said that the name of the cat was Juanita and that she spoke Russian.

I yelled at the television, "No, stupid, that's a girl at school! My cat is Pip, and she speaks Spanish!"

Mom came into the family room. "Singing with the radio? Well, you have to stop. It's dessert time!"

I got up and followed her to the kitchen. I stared at two popsicles that were frozen tomatoes on chopsticks. I went to bed without dessert and cried myself to sleep.

The next day after school I ran over to Sr. Medina's. There was a reporter on his hands and knees.

"What are you doing?" I asked.

He looked up, surprised. "Well, I'm looking for a camera lens. Dropped it yesterday. Boy, was that some crowd."

I looked at Sr. Medina's house. "Is he home?"

"Home?" the reporter asked, rising to his feet. "That Medina guy moved out; he's gone."

"What do you mean — gone!" I almost screamed.

"Just that. He's gone." He snapped his fingers. "He moved out last night and took his cat with him."

Chills ran down my back. I shivered, buried my face in my hands, and started to cry.

"Hey," the reporter asked. "What's wrong?"

I started running up the block, thinking, "Poor Sr. Medina. He didn't do anything. He's a good man." But I ran back when I thought of that woman who had squealed to the reporters. I wanted revenge. Anger boiled in my veins.

She was watering her lawn and cackling with laughter to herself. I bit my lip and made a fist. I crossed the street, yanked the hose from her, and sprayed her up and down.

"You evil witch," I yelled. "You don't know anything about secrets. You're nothing but a sour old snoop."

I sprayed her and for a second I thought she might start shrinking into a puddle of nothing, like the evil witch from *The Wizard of Oz*. Instead, she yelled at me to stop, which I did. I didn't look back.

CHAPTER
7

Pip didn't come home that night. She didn't come home the next day or that week or the week after. Every day I ran down to Sr. Medina's, hoping that he would be reading on the porch. There were only shadows there, and newspapers piling up.

I cried, moped around the house, and kept to myself. I started a journal: *Lonely Days Without Pip*. I filled its pages in no time, and then hid it in my room, with a big white label stuck to the front: SECRETS. PLEASE DO NOT READ. THIS MEANS YOU!

My parents were no help. They were as crazy as ever.

Dad knew that something was troubling me, and to cheer me up he said, "Hey, let's play catch." In the front yard we tossed a tennis ball back and forth, but, tired and bored, I threw my sweater onto our bush and went inside. Dad thought the sweater was me. He threw the ball, and the ball bounced back. I had never seen him so happy.

But one rainy Saturday was the best day of my life. I was in my room playing checkers by myself when I heard a "meow, meow, meow." I got off my bed and looked outside. A black cat was sitting under a tree and looking right at me. I opened the window and shouted, "Poor gatito, come on in."

The cat raced to my window and, after she thought about doing it, leaped to my windowsill and scratched for a pawhold.

I pulled her in, dried her off with my robe, and cuddled her on my bed. I pressed my nose to her nose. "You're cute."

"Meow," she said, "meow, meow, meow."

"What's your name?"

"Meow."

I stared at her and thought that she looked like Pip, except she was black and Pip was white (dirty white, really).

"You look like my old cat," I said. "You really do."

The black cat licked a paw and then looked up, "Oui, je suis Pip."*

My hair stood on end. "Did you say you're Pip, my Pip?"

"Oui, Graciela.

"You're back?"

"Oui."

I couldn't believe it. I hugged this new Pip, almost cried, and then quickly pulled back.

* Yes, I am Pip. (French)

73

"But why are you black, and how did you learn French?"

Pip closed her eyes as she shook her head and said, "C'est un secret."*

"A secret?" I asked. I was going to ask Pip what it was but remembered Sr. Medina. I had no right to ask. It was between them, not me. After all, a secret is a secret.

At that moment Mom came in wearing a hat hung with all sorts of plastic fruits.

"Why are you wearing that hat?" I asked.

"Because it's lunchtime, Graciela." She laughed and slapped her knees with both hands. "And Pip, I have tomato leftovers for you."

She left, reminding me to put on my socks before I came to the table. Pip and I looked at one another and rolled our eyes toward the ceiling.

"She didn't even notice you changed colors," I said. "Mom is so weird. And she doesn't know you can speak two languages."

* It's a secret. (French)

75

"Tres," Pip said. "Cuatro, cinco, seis."*

"Six languages?" I yelled, but was quick enough to cover my mouth.

Pip winked at me. "Más."**

"More than six?" I slapped my cheek and let my mouth fall open, utterly amazed. I was in love with the smartest cat in the whole world.

* Three . . . four, five, six.
** More.

GLOSSARY

Adiós. — Good-bye.

Buenas noches. — Good night.

casa — house

chisme — gossip

chorizo — Mexican sausage

Claro que sí. — Of course.

¿Cómo está usted? ¿Cómo estás? — How are you?

¿Cómo te ha ido? — How have you been?

¿Cómo te llamas? — What's your name?

¿Cómo te va? — How are you doing?

Díme. — Tell me.

¿Dónde estás? — Where are you?

¿Estás triste? — Are you sad?

fantástico — fantastic

fiesta — party, celebration

¡Fíjate! — Pay attention!

gatito — kitty

Hola. — Hello.

huachinango — red snapper (a fish)

loca — crazy

más — more

mi amiga — my friend (girl)

Míra. — Look.

muy bien — very well

No importa. — It doesn't matter.

No sé. — I don't know.

No te preocupes. — Don't worry.

No te puedo decir. — I can't tell you.

¡Órale! — All right!

Perdón. — I'm sorry.

el periódico — the newspaper

por favor — please

¿Por qué no? — Why not?

Qué bonito está el día. — It's a beautiful day.

Qué bueno. — That's good.

¿Qué dices? — What did you say?

Qué lástima. — What a shame.

¿Qué tal? — What's up?

Quiero más. — I want more.

un regalo — a gift

sí — yes

Siéntate. — Sit down.

Tengo hambre. — I'm hungry.

tres, cuatro, cinco, seis — three, four, five, six

tu abuelo — your grandfather

Vamos a comer. — Let's go eat.

Ven acá. — Come here.

¿Verdad? — Isn't that true?

la vieja — the old lady